How Many Donkeys?

An Arabic Counting Tale

Retold from a Saudi folktale by

Margaret Read MacDonald and **Nadia Jameel Taibah**

Illustrated by **Carol Liddiment**

Albert Whitman & Company, Morton Grove, Illinois

Thanks to the children of Natches Trail Elementary, American International School of Guangzhou, American International School of Dhaka, and Bonn International School for help in perfecting this text. It was exciting to learn that kids liked to repeat the Arabic numbers while I was reading! And it was good to find out that several classes then went to the web to discover more about counting in Arabic.

And of course thank you to Nadia Jameel Taibah, who contributed the story and checked every detail for accuracy.—M.R.M.

To my mother, Zain—N.J.T.

In memory of my dad, Jim—C.L.

Library of Congress Cataloging-in-Publication Data

MacDonald, Margaret Read, 1940-
How many donkeys? : an Arabic counting tale / retold by Margaret Read MacDonald and Nadia Jameel Taibah ;
illustrations by Carol Liddiment.
p. cm.
Summary: When Jouha counts the ten donkeys carrying his dates to market, he repeatedly forgets to count the one he is riding on, causing him great consternation. Includes numbers written out in Arabic and in English transliteration, as well as the numerals one through ten, and a note on the origins and other versions of the story.
ISBN 978-0-8075-3424-3
[1. Arabs—Folklore. 2. Folklore—Arab countries. 3. Counting.] I. Taibah, Nadia Jameel. II. Liddiment, Carol, ill. III. Title.
PZ8.M1755Ho 2009 398.209174—dc22 [E] 2008056047

Published in 2009 by Albert Whitman & Company, 6340 Oakton Street, Morton Grove, Illinois 60053-2723.

Printed in China.
10 9 8 7 6 5 4 3 2 1

The design is by Carol Gildar.

For more information about Albert Whitman & Company, please visit our web site at www.albertwhitman.com.

Saudi storyteller Nadia Jameel Taibah heard this story from her aunt Salha.

Jouha (*JOU-huh*—ou as in *could)* is a wise fool much beloved in Middle Eastern folklore. These tales are told in Turkey about Nasr-din Hodja and in Iran about the Mullah. Egypt calls him Goha. Wherever he is found and under whatever name, his tales are always a mix of wisdom and foolishness, with trickster elements tossed in. In this book Jouha puts on his foolishness hat. Variants of this tale can be found in *Nine in a Line* by Ann Kirn (W. W. Norton, 1966) [Egypt], in *Goha the Wise Fool* by Denys Johnson-Davies (Philomel, 2005) [Egypt], and in *Once the Hodja* by Alice Kelsey (McKay, 1943) [Turkey].

The tale is found widely in folk literature under *Motif J2022 Numbskull cannot find ass he is sitting on.* My *Storyteller's Sourcebook* cites versions from Syria, Armenia, Turkey, and North Africa. The Iraqi dancer Farid Zodan recently told me a very similar Jouha tale well known in his family. Antti Aarne's *The Types of the Folktale* cites under *Type 1288A* variants from Spain, Germany, Italy, Hungary, Serbo-Croatia, and Puerto Rico. For a similar tale, *J2031 Counting wrong by not counting oneself,* Stith Thompson's *Motif-Index of Folk-Literature* cites tales from England, Turkey, Switzerland, India, and Indonesia. ***M.R.M.***

Arabic is written from right to left, hence the order of the Arabic at the bottom of the pages. There are a variety of Arabic dialects. The pronunciations below are based on Modern Standard Arabic, which is the language of books and formal instruction used all over the Arabic world.

You can hear me say the numbers from one to ten on this web site: www.margaretreadmacdonald.com. ***N.J.T.***

1 **Wahid** wah HEHD (a as in *father)*
2 **Ithnan** ihth NAHN
3 **Thalatha** tha LA thuh (a as in *hat)*
4 **Arba'a** AHR ba uh
5 **Khamsa** KAHM suh
6 **Sitta** SIHT tuh
7 **Sab'a** SAHB uh
8 **Thamanya** thah MAN ih yuh
9 **Tis'a** TIHS uh
10 **Ashara** AH shah rah

Jouha is loading donkeys
with dates to sell at the market.
But how many donkeys are here?

عشرة	تسعة	ثمانية	سبعة	ستة
Ashara	Tis'a	Thamanya	Sab'a	Sitta
10 ١٠	9 ٩	8 ٨	7 ٧	6 ٦

"Son, help me count."

"Wahid . . . that's one. Ithnan . . . two. Thalatha . . . three. Arba'a . . . four. Khamsa . . . five. Sitta . . . six. Sab'a . . . seven. Thamanya . . . eight. Tis'a . . . nine. Ashara . . . ten.

Ten donkeys, Baba. Have a good trip!"

خمسة	أربعة	ثلاثة	إثنان	واحد
Khamsa	Arba'a	Thalatha	Ithnan	Wahid
5 ٥	4 ٤	3 ٣	2 ٢	1 ١

Over the sandhills,
through sandy valleys.
A long, long way to the market.

"Ten donkeys
going to market.
I am a lucky man!"

"Ten donkeys . . .
going to . . . WAIT!

Wahid . . . that's one.
Ithnan . . . two.
Thalatha . . . three.
Arba'a . . . four.
Khamsa . . . five.
Sitta . . . six.
Sab'a . . . seven.
Thamanya . . . eight.
Tis'a . . . nine. Tis'a! NINE?

A donkey is lost! I am an unlucky man!"

"COUNT AGAIN, JOUHA!"

"Wahid. Ithnan. Thalatha. Arba'a. Khamsa. Sitta. Sab'a. Thamanya. Tis'a. Ashara—ten!

عشرة	تسعة	ثمانية	سبعة	ستة
Ashara	Tis'a	Thamanya	Sab'a	Sitta
10 ١٠	9 ٩	8 ٨	7 ٧	6 ٦

"The lost donkey is back!
I am a lucky man!"

"Water ahead. A good place to stop.
My donkeys can rest for a while.

Oh, no—I see NINE!
One ran off again!
I am an unlucky man!"

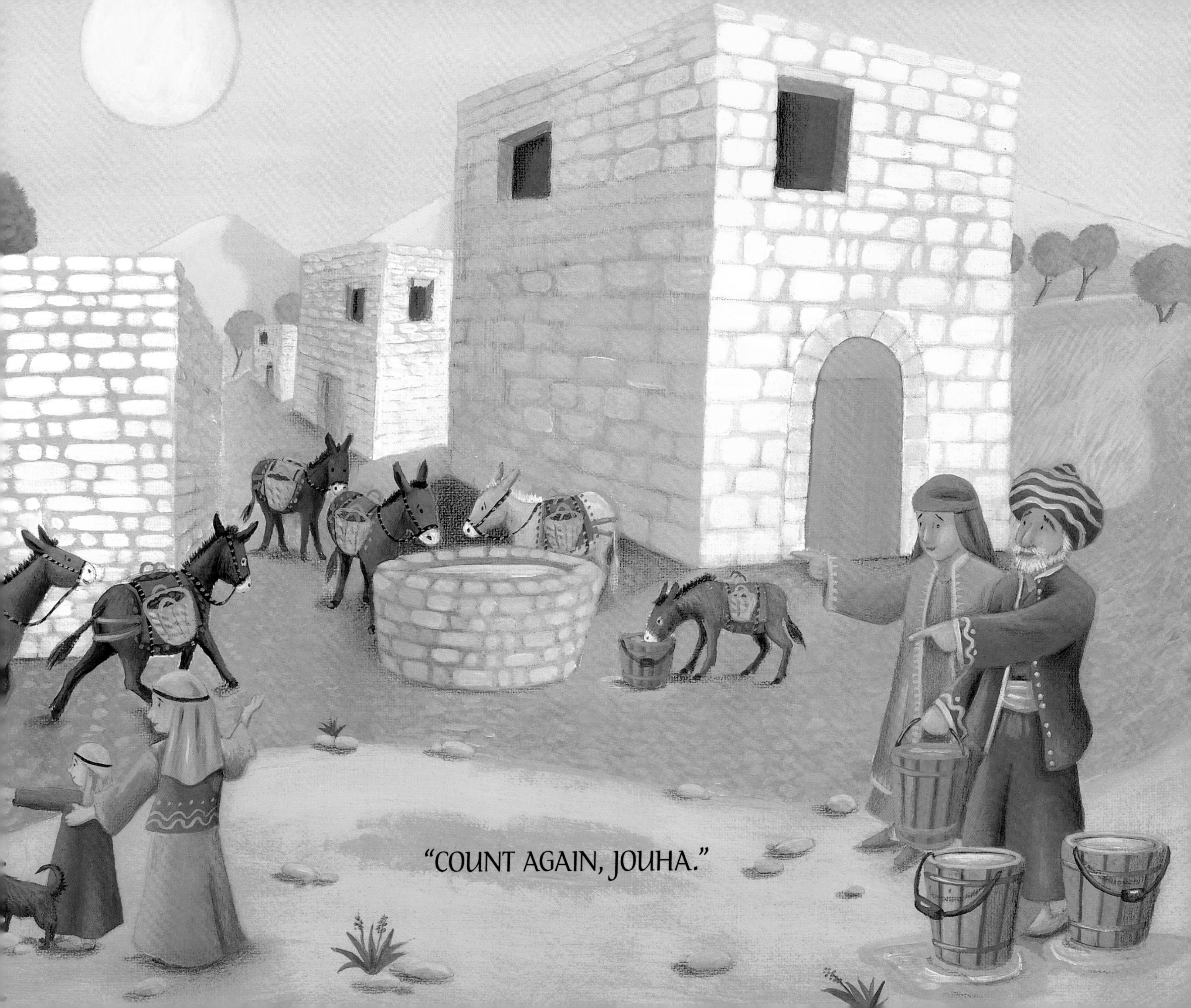

“COUNT AGAIN, JOUHA.”

“I’ll get off and count again.

“Wahid . . . one.
Ithnan . . . two.
Thalatha . . . three.
Arba’a . . . four.
Khamsa . . . five.

خمسة
Khamsa
5 ٥
أربعة
Arba'a
4 ٤
ثلاثة
Thalatha
3 ٣
إثنان
Ithnan
2 ٢
واحد
Wahid
1 ١

"Sitta . . . six.
Sab'a . . . seven.
Thamanya . . . eight.
Tis'a . . . nine.
Ashara! ten!

“The lost donkey came back! I am a lucky man!”

"Ten donkeys with dates . . . to sell at the market.
I'd better count them again.

Wahid . . . one. Ithnan . . . two.
Thalatha . . . three. Arba'a . . . four.
Khamsa . . . five. Sitta . . . six.
Sab'a . . . seven. Thamanya . . . eight.
Tis'a . . . Tis'a? NINE!

“One lost again!
I am an unlucky man.”

"COUNT AGAIN, JOUHA!"

عشرة	تسعة	ثمانية	سبعة	ستة
Ashara	Tis'a	Thamanya	Sab'a	Sitta
10 ١٠	9 ٩	8 ٨	7 ٧	6 ٦

“Wahid . . . that’s one. Ithnan . . . two.
Thalatha . . . three. Arba’a . . . four.
Khamsa . . . five. Sitta . . . six. Sab’a . . . seven.
Thamanya . . . eight. Tis’a . . . nine. Ashara . . . ten.
Ashara! Ten!

The donkey is back! I am a lucky man!”

"Now I can sell my dates at the market. I am a happy man!"

"I won't lose a donkey on my way home.
Now I know what I did wrong.
If I RIDE on a donkey, a donkey escapes!
If I WALK, they cannot run away."

"It's better to walk than to lose a donkey.
I've learned that lesson today."

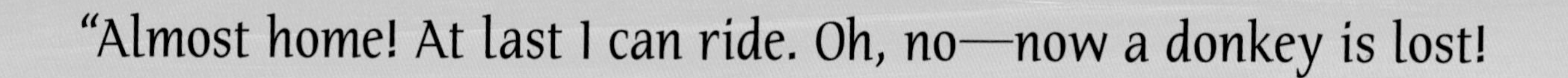

“Almost home! At last I can ride. Oh, no—now a donkey is lost!

Wahid . . . that’s one. Ithnan . . . two. Thalatha . . . three.
Arba’a . . . four. Khamsa . . . five. Sitta . . . six. Sab’a . . . seven.
Thamanya . . . eight. TIS’A! Nine.

“I’ve come home with just *nine.* I am an unlucky man!”

"Let me count, Baba." His son helps him count.

"Wahid. Ithnan. Thalatha. Arba'a. Khamsa. Sitta. Sab'a. Thamanya. Tis'a. Ashara! Ten!

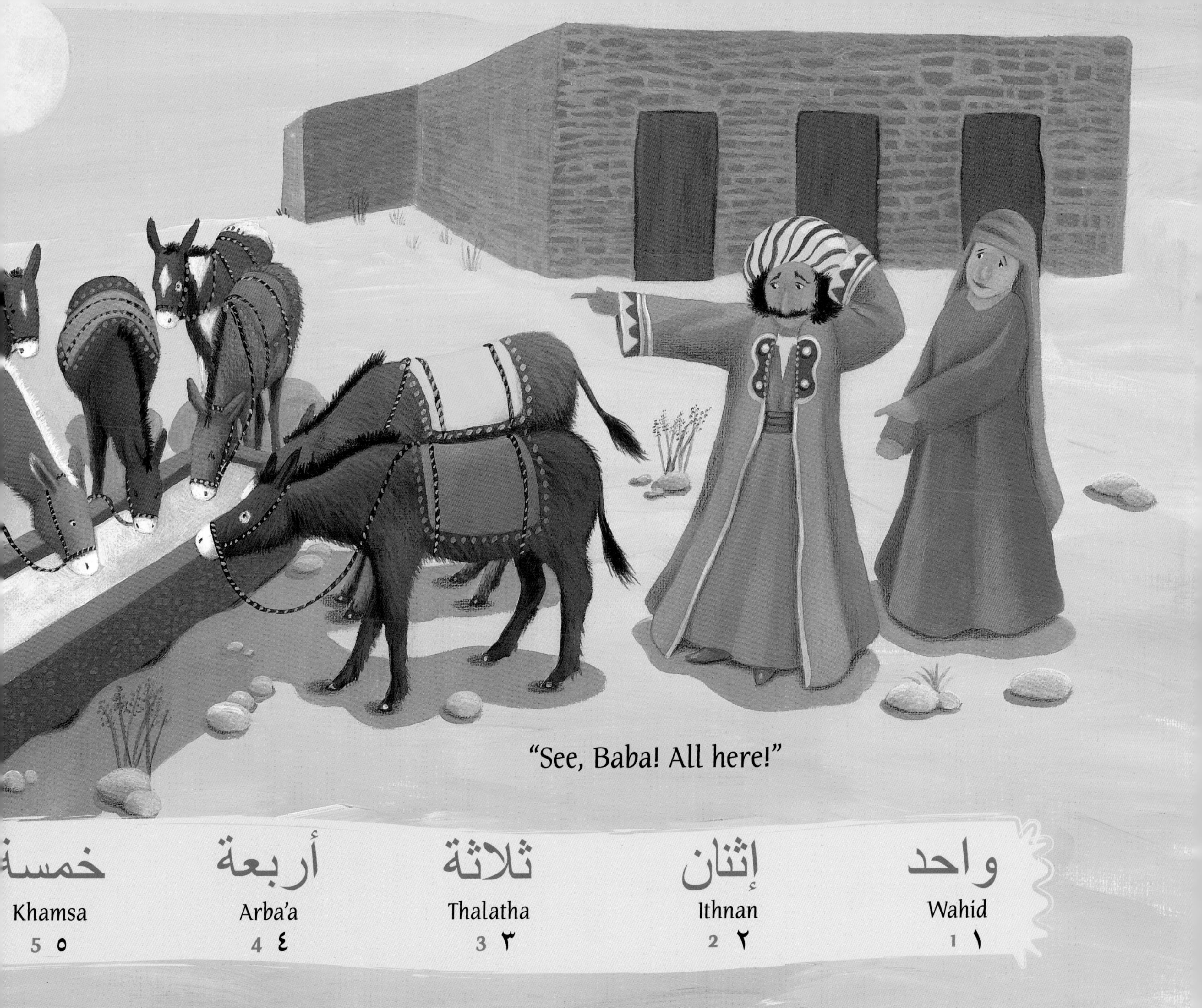
“See, Baba! All here!”
خمسة
Khamsa
5 ٥
أربعة
Arba’a
4 ٤
ثلاثة
Thalatha
3 ٣
إثنان
Ithnan
2 ٢
واحد
Wahid
1 ١

“A clever son! My lost donkey is found! I am a lucky man!”